Just Wait And See

Written and illustrated by

N. E. Lamy

www.NELamyAuthor.Wordpress.com

For my mum, who always told me I'd be an author someday.

And also for everyone who reads this book, no matter how young or old you may be.

Dream on - You can do it!

Just Wait And See!

"Ezzie, dinner's ready," called Mummy Rabbit, through the open kitchen window. But Ezzie was so lost in her wonderful daydream that she didn't hear.

"Ezmeralda Rabbit!" yelled Mummy Rabbit again, slowly losing her patience.

"Just a minute," came Ezzie's voice from the very bottom of the garden.

She took one last look out across the sparkling brook to the field beyond – a field filled with luscious looking lettuces.

"Why don't we ever eat lettuces?" Ezzie asked that evening at the dinner table.

"Because they don't grow on this side of the brook," replied Mummy Rabbit. "And even though the brook is very shallow, rabbits don't like getting wet."

"Lettuces used to grow on our side of the brook a long time ago," Grandpa Rabbit interrupted.

"When I was a young buck, we'd have lettuces for dinner every Sunday," he continued wistfully. "I can still remember how delicious they taste!"

"I'm going to jump over the brook and eat lettuces," announced Ezzie the next morning.

Ezzie's little brother, Frankie, giggled thinking it was a joke, whilst Daddy Rabbit concealed a snort of laughter from behind his newspaper.

"That's impossible Ezzie," he said gently. "No rabbit has ever jumped over the brook before."
"Rabbits can't jump over the brook," Mummy Rabbit added looking concerned.

Ezzie smiled. "Just because no rabbit has ever done it before, doesn't mean it can't be done," she said. "Just wait and see."

"What are you doing Ezzie? Come and play with us!" called Baz from across the playground.

"I'm practising," answered Ezzie, as she bounded quickly across the grass and jumped high into the air, stretching out as far as she could.

"I'm going to jump over the brook and eat lettuces," she gasped, out of breath.

"Very funny," laughed Baz. "No rabbit has ever jumped over the brook."
"Just because no rabbit has ever done it before, doesn't mean it can't be done," Ezzie smiled. "Just wait and see."

That night, before she fell asleep, Ezzie imagined what it would feel like to jump over the brook and eat a lettuce for the very first time.

She closed her eyes and pictured herself jumping high and far, using her strong legs to spring from the bank of the brook.

She saw the water flash by beneath her and she felt the thud as she landed on the other side, right in amongst all those juicy looking lettuces.

She imagined what a lettuce might taste like, how succulent and sweet the leaves might be and she drifted off to sleep with a smile.

For the next few weeks, Ezzie rehearsed in her mind what it would feel like to jump over the brook and she practised for real whenever she could.

She had even started leaping over the hedge into next door's garden to see how high and how far she could jump.

Frankie thought this was very brave, as Mr Badger, who lived next door, didn't like rabbits.

In fact, come to think of it, he didn't like much of anything at all.

One time, Ezzie cleared the hedge and jumped so far she landed right in the middle of Mr Badger's flowerbed.

"Oops", thought Ezzie, as she tried to jump back over the hedge without being seen.

Unfortunately, Mr Badger had been watching from his window and came rushing out of his house, shouting and waving his walking stick crossly.

"Get out of my flowerbed," he ordered.
After that, Ezzie had to be very careful about where she practised her jumping.

One day at school, Mrs Buckley asked the class to write about something they were going to do during the holidays.

"I am jumping over the brook and eating yummy lettuces," Ezzie wrote.

Ezzie loved writing those words. They made her smile. She liked how they made her feel as if she could do anything she imagined.

"Very neat handwriting Ezzie," said Mrs Buckley as she handed back her work, "although this wasn't meant to be a made up story. No rabbit can really jump over the brook," she added in a kindly way.

"Just wait and see," thought Ezzie to herself with a smile.

And then one day, Ezzie knew it was time. She'd been training hard, she'd practised in her mind and she was ready.

It was a beautiful day. The brook was sparkling in the morning sunlight and the lettuces on the other side looked absolutely scrumptious.

Ezzie knew she could do it, no matter what anyone else said. She took a deep breath and began running and hopping as fast as she could.

Just at that moment, Mummy Rabbit came out into the garden and shrieked as she caught a glimpse of Ezzie hurtling towards the edge of the brook.

Daddy Rabbit, Grandpa Rabbit and Frankie came running. They all watched open mouthed as Ezzie leapt from the bank, out across the water.

Mummy Rabbit gasped in shock as Ezzie soared through the air.

Time slowed down as Ezzie jumped. She kept her eyes firmly on the lettuces beyond and she didn't look down at the splashing water below.

And then, just as she had imagined all those times, she felt herself coming back down to earth with a thud.

She'd done it! She'd jumped over the brook. A huge roar of applause erupted from behind her.

"You did it Ezzie, you really did it!" whooped Frankie.

“Well I never!” exclaimed Grandpa Rabbit.
“If I hadn’t seen it with my own eyes, I wouldn’t have believed it,” said Daddy Rabbit in amazement.

Mummy Rabbit was far too shocked to speak.

As for Ezzie, she was hopping for joy in amongst the lettuces.

"I did it!" she shouted. "I knew I could do it. I just knew it!"

And with that, she took her first ever nibble of a lettuce and a huge smile spread across her face.

It tasted even more delicious than she could ever have imagined.

The End

Thank you for reading